MW01100849

The *BAD MANOR GIRLS*
Save Picturia

Story by Diane Johnson
Pictures by Catherine Anne Tower,
Lauren Kate Johnson, and
Patricia and Robin DeWitt

Acknowledgements

With thanks to Olivia, my first grandchild, for the inspiration to publish;

my mother, Pamela, for typing the handwritten manuscript;

the eclectic characters from the original Bad Manor;

community advocates, for making the world a better place; and

Eckhart Tolle, the Master of Presence.

About the Illustrations

When I wrote the story in the early 1970s, I was living in a communal house with four other students. Susan Read, one of my roommates, drew the original illustrations. I was unable to use Susan's drawings due to copyright considerations.

In 2021, I contacted an author who had recently published a children's story that she had written in the 1960s. Her illustrator, award-winning BC artist Catherine Anne Tower (grand-niece of Emily Carr), created some of the illustrations (pages 3-7, 15, 21, 27, 28, 33, 40-42) for *The Bad Manor Girls Save Picturia.*

Lauren Kate Johnson, devoted wife and mother of three (my amazing daughter-in-law), contributed several images (pages 11, 18, 30, 31).

The additional illustrations (Cover, pages 8, 12, 13, 17, 19, 23, 34, 36, 37, 39) were provided by FriesenPress illustrators, Patricia and Robin DeWitt.

I hope you enjoy the variety of styles.

Diane Johnson

Once upon a time, there was an old, old house on an old, old street, just on the outskirts of an old, old city. The city was named Picturia because it was a beautiful place with miles of natural coastline and fresh, clean air. The street was lined with magnificent trees, unique gardens, and intriguing homes. The house had a sign above its door that read *BAD MANOR*

Five girls lived in the house. No one was quite sure how long the girls had lived in *Bad Manor*, but most thought they had come to attend the local university. One thing everyone knew for sure was that since the girls had moved there, strange people went to the house at odd times of the day, and folks who lived nearby noticed strange lights and sounds coming from the manor at all hours. Not surprisingly, the *Bad Manor Girls* were more than what they seemed!

To the neighbours, *Genie* was a friendly little student with bright green eyes and glasses who was liked by everyone she met. But inside *Bad Manor*, she was *Queen of the Eye-eyes*, and she had power over all sight. *Queen Genie* could change the way things *looked*.

4

Marianna, another girl who lived at the manor, had long dark hair and was very lively. Most of the time, she was with *Allisanna*, who had long purple hair and liked to wear hats. They always had a lot of fun. *Marianna and Allisanna* were the *Sisters of Ear-ee-land*, and they possessed power over all sound. The sisters could change the way things *sounded*.

From the *Land of Lip-er-ary* had come the fair-haired *Duchess*. All taste and smell were in her power, yet she was no taller than *Genie! Duchess* could change the way things *tasted* and the way things *smelled*.

Finally, there was the red-haired *Katrine*, who was a bit wild but was very good at making things. Her original home was *Feel-ee-ter*, and her father, the *King of the Velveetians*, had given her power over all touch. *Princess Katrine* could change the way things *felt*.

Genie, Marianna, Allisanna, Duchess, and Katrine had a pretty Persian cat with rainbow whiskers named Pussycat. Pussycat was very wise and lived a fuller life than most people. She never spoke unless it was absolutely necessary. To anyone other than the five girls, she was just an ordinary kitty with a sweet face and a soothing *purrr*.

THE HAZE

BAD MANOR

The year the girls moved into *Bad Manor*, Picturia was as beautiful as ever, but a terrible plight had befallen the inhabitants. *Ig,* the *Evil One*, was using *The HAZE* on Picturia's unsuspecting citizens.

Ig was a spoiler, and that's just what he wanted to do. He wanted to spoil Picturia. He wanted to pour waste into Picturia Bay, pollute Picturia's fresh, clean air, and cut down Picturia's magnificent trees. But before *Ig* and his forces from *Dulland* could swoop in and spoil the city, Picturia's citizens first had to be dulled by *The HAZE.*

Already, *The HAZE* was making the residents feel drowsy and distracted. People walked with their eyes down. They did not notice the sky or the ocean. They did not hear the birds or the waves. They did not taste their food or smell the scent of blossoms in spring. They did not feel the warmth from their fireplaces. In fact, most folks hardly noticed anything at all. Under *The HAZE* spell, they were barely awake and barely aware. Soon *Ig* would summon his *Forces of Ig-norance* and ruin Picturia forever.

The five *Bad Manor Girls* had noticed the effect *The HAZE* was having on Picturia's inhabitants. They knew about *Ig's* evil intentions, and they had gathered at *Bad Manor* to try to break the spell. A special wake-up event was about to begin, and Picturia would experience many surprises!

It was Monday morning when Mr. and Mrs. Pottlebog went out to the store to buy pillows for the kitchen table; they had been so tired lately, they seemed to fall asleep anywhere. As they passed *Bad Manor,* Mrs. Pottlebog happened to look up. There, in the upstairs window, was an *enormous green eye!*

The eye blinked and turned purple. Old Mrs. Pottlebog was so surprised, she jumped three feet in the air. Mr. Pottlebog had never seen his wife jump so high.

"Look at that!" said Mrs. Pottlebog, pointing at the eye.

"Look at that!" said Mr. Pottlebog, pointing at his wife.

In downtown Picturia, strange things were happening. Overnight, City Hall had been painted with bright pink and purple stripes!

"Look at that!" exclaimed the mayor when he noticed the brightly-colored building.

When the teachers arrived at Picturia High School that morning, they were shocked to *see* that the men had grown brilliant orange beards and the women now had bright purple streaks in their hair!

"Look at that," was heard in every classroom.

The skipper of a sailboat on Picturia Bay noticed that the ocean was not its usual grey; the water was turquoise, and he *saw* fat green piggies swimming behind the boat!

"Look *at those* **pigs!"** he exclaimed.

Sail Away

Later in the day, a silver rain began to fall. The drops turned to crystals, making everything glitter. Children asked if they could play outside. At first, their parents wanted to keep them indoors, but soon all the little girls and boys were calling their friends to join them in the sparkling rain.

Picturia was even more beautiful with sparkles, and everywhere could be heard cries of *"Look there!"* and *"Oh, **look**, isn't that gorgeous?"* Many people were paying attention, and when the rain stopped, more people were alert. But there were more surprises coming.

Queen Genie put her glasses back on, and the *bright purple eye* disappeared from the upstairs window of *Bad Manor.*

By Tuesday morning, the silver rain had faded. The pink and purple stripes, orange beards, purple streaks, and green piggies were gone!

Mr. Pottlebog went down the road to *Bad Manor* to see if the eye was still there, because Mrs. Pottlebog made him go.

"Well?" she said when he returned. "Is it there?"

"No," said Mr. Pottlebog. "There's an *enormous ear*."

In downtown Picturia, whenever a car approached a stop sign, an alarm clock rang. Every time a driver honked their horn, the cars made animal noises. Some grunted, some whinnied, some hee-hawed, and some barked. The city sounded like a barnyard before feeding time.

18

When little Janet Jinglejoy went to play in the woods with her friends, she *heard* the sounds of a carnival. Children laughed and screamed on the Tilt-a-Whirl, music blared from the Ferris wheel, and someone shouted, "Hot Dogs. Candy Floss. Toffee apples!"

"Listen to that," she said. Janet and her friends searched through the trees, but there was no carnival to be found.

That afternoon, as Ms. Pricklepuss walked along the seashore with her sweetheart, Peter Pickingslip, she was certain she could *hear* the sounds of a symphony coming from the ocean waves.

"Listen to that!" she exclaimed happily.

The strange happenings also reached Mrs. Pottlebog inside her house! She could *hear* old rock and roll tunes, and Mr. Pottlebog found her dancing around the kitchen, waving her hands in the air, and singing, "Roll Over Beethoven."

The number of times, ***"Listen to that,"*** was heard on Tuesday was amazing!

Back at *Bad Manor,* sisters *Marianna and Allisanna* brushed their hair over their ears and grinned at each other, and the *enormous ear* disappeared from the upstairs window.

When Wednesday morning arrived, and alarm clocks rang, Picturians wondered if they were hearing stop signs. Then they hopped out of bed as fast as they could. They didn't want to miss anything.

Every morning, Mrs. Pottlebog made breakfast for her husband. Every morning, he had oatmeal porridge. This morning, he dropped his spoon after the first bite.

"Good gracious," Mr. Pottlebog declared. *"My porridge **tastes** like black cherry ice cream!"*

Mrs. Pottlebog smiled. Her husband hadn't been so sweet to her in a long time. But, when she sipped her tea, it definitely *tasted* like raspberry pie.

"Hmm," said Mrs. Pottlebog. "Hmm."

Later, Mrs. Pottlebog bravely went out to check on *Bad Manor*, and there in the upstairs window was a *giant pair of lips and a nose.*

"Just as I thought," she said. "Hmm."

Next door to the Pottlebogs, Ms. Pricklepuss baked a fresh batch of chocolate chip cookies—her favorite recipe—and took some over to her darling, Peter.

"Taste these," he later said to a friend. *"They look like chocolate chip cookies, but they **taste** completely different!"*

Ms. Pricklepuss was very surprised when she received a note from Peter, thanking her for the scrumptious *carrot* cookies.

At City Hall, the mayor opened his window and took a deep breath. **"Smell that?"** he asked his assistant.

"Apple blossoms, and not an orchard in sight!" she exclaimed.

27

In the afternoon, Janet Jinglejoy and her friends rushed to the woods, hoping to finally find the carnival. This time, they could *smell* buttered popcorn and hamburgers with fried onions!

"*Can you* **smell** *that?*" they asked each other, but although they searched and searched, they could not find the carnival.

Some people in Picturia noticed a fishy scent blowing in from the sea. "*Do you* **smell** *salmon?*" they asked.

But then the wind changed direction, and they said, "**Smell** *that steak!*"

Others exclaimed, "**Smell** *that homemade bread!*"

That evening, *Duchess* smiled, and the *giant pair of lips and a nose* disappeared from the upstairs window of *Bad Manor*.

On Thursday morning, a *large hand* appeared in the upstairs window. But, before anything else could happen, the girls of the manor had a visitor.

"Let me in," ordered the tall, dark, sleepy-looking man at the door. "Let me in! I am the mayor of Picturia, and it has come to my attention that—"

"Come in, come in," invited the girls politely.

"All this commotion is your fault," snarled the man with an evil sneer. "*GET OUT! Leave Picturia, and never . . . come . . .*" Before he could finish speaking, he fell asleep in the nearest and softest chair!

The astonished girls could not believe their eyes and ears. How could the mayor of such a beautiful place as Picturia be so rude and then fall asleep so quickly when so many extraordinary things were happening in his town?

Meanwhile, *Pussycat* was getting ready to go out to a neighbourhood party, but first, she jumped into *Allisanna's* lap and touched her cheek.

"*Ig,*" whispered the Persian, between *purrrs*.

"*Ig!*" exclaimed *Marianna and Allisanna* together.

"*Ig,*" said *Genie,* opening her eyes wide. "*Ig* is pretending to be the mayor. We should have known by his evil sneer."

"*The HAZE* must have affected *Ig,* too," concluded *Duchess,* looking at the sleeping *Evil One.* "Quick! If we combine our powers, we can send him back to *Dulland.* With luck, he will stay asleep and never threaten anyone again!"

The girls joined hands, and in an instant, the chair was empty, and *Ig* was safely asleep in *Dulland!*

A moment later, there was a knock at the door. On the porch was a pleasant-looking red-haired man in a blue suit jacket.

"I am sorry to bother you," he said. "I am the mayor of Picturia. Your neighbour, Mrs. Pottlebog, has reported that strange objects have been appearing in your upstairs window, and she thinks they are related to the astounding events of the last few days."

The girls looked at one another. They did not want to confuse the mayor with tales of *Eye-eyes and Ear-ee-land,* so they explained that *Genie* was studying to be a teacher; the big eye, ear, lips, nose, and hand were models for one of her classes.

The mayor seemed satisfied and relieved. After apologizing again for the interruption, he left. But, as he stepped onto the sidewalk, instead of walking, he *felt* like he was sliding. In fact, he could actually skate down the sidewalk!

*"Try sliding on this sidewalk; it **feels** like ice,"* he called to anyone he passed as he slid all the way back to City Hall.

For the rest of the morning, all the roads and sidewalks *felt* like ice; no cars or bikes could be used. Everyone had to slide from place to place.

Mr. and Mrs. Pottlebog went for a slide instead of their daily walk, and the children of Picturia had sliding races and bouncing contests.

*"Try bouncing; it **feels** wonderful!"* shouted Granny Flopper, having as much fun as everyone else. She wasn't afraid of falling, because when she fell, she bounced right back up again, as good as new!

In his home on Picturia Bay, Mr. Jinglejoy lit a fire in his fireplace, but rather than the warmth of the flames, he could *feel* a cool breeze blowing.

*"Can you **feel** that cold draft?"* he asked his wife.

He picked up some wood to stoke the fire, but when he touched the surface of the cedar log, he *felt* wooden cheekbones and a nose!

*"**Feel** this log!"* he exclaimed.

Inspired, Mr. Jinglejoy found a knife and some gloves, and started whittling away at the wood. In a short time, he had produced a carving that looked like his wife's sweet face! Mr. Jinglejoy proudly showed his creation to an astonished Mrs. Jinglejoy.

That afternoon, Mrs. La-di-da walked barefoot on the lush carpet of her mansion on the other side of the bay. Instead of lovely, plush softness, the carpet *felt* hard and bumpy.

*"This carpet **feels** like a rocky beach!"* she cried in dismay. "Ow, I hurt my toe!"

Satisfied, *Princess Katrine* nodded her head, and the *large hand* disappeared from the upstairs window of *Bad Manor.*

By the end of the week, everyone in Picturia had used the spell-breaking words, *look, listen, smell, taste,* or *feel.* Certainly, all had noticed something unusual, and all were paying attention.

On the weekend, Mrs. Pottlebog made pancakes for breakfast. The pancakes were not Mr. Pottlebog's usual oatmeal porridge, and they did not taste like black cherry ice cream, but Mr. Pottlebog noticed that they were delicious just the same!

Janet Jinglejoy and her friends never did find the carnival, but they did find some wonderful climbing trees.

Eventually, City Hall got a new coat of paint, and hair with purple streaks became a trend at Picturia High.

Mrs. Pottlebog became a Rolling Stones fan, and the mayor went skating every Sunday.

Mr. Jinglejoy became a carver of some renown, and the newlywed Pickingslips agreed that with the right companion, walking together beside the ocean was very enjoyable, even without the symphony.

Picturians were once again awake and aware. Picturia's natural coastline, clean, fresh air, and magnificent trees were safe!

Strange objects no longer appeared in the upstairs window of *Bad Manor.* Strange people still went to the house at odd times of the day, and strange lights and sounds still came from the manor at all hours, but people said, "You can expect such things from university students!"

Someday, *Ig* may wake and use *The HAZE* on your town, but don't worry! The *Bad Manor Girls* will be nearby. If you *see* silver rain or *hear* the symphony at the seashore, if you *taste* carrot cookies, *smell* homemade bread on the wind, or *feel* ice on the sidewalk, you will know that you are awake and aware; *The HAZE* cannot affect you.

You can be sure of this because on an old, old street, just on the outskirts of an old, old city, somewhere, somehow, there will always be five girls with special powers, a pretty Persian cat, and an old, old house with a sign above its door that reads, **BAD MANOR**.

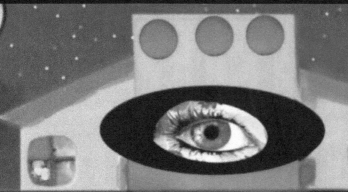

FriesenPress

One Printers Way
Altona, MB R0G 0B0
Canada

www.friesenpress.com

Illustrators:
Catherine Anne Tower
Pages: 3-7, 15, 21, 27, 28, 33, 40-42

Lauren Kate Johnson
Pages: 11, 18, 30, 31

Patricia and Robin DeWitt
Pages: Cover, 8, 12, 13, 17, 19, 23, 34, 36, 37, 39

ISBN
978-1-03-914798-0 (Hardcover)
978-1-03-914797-3 (Paperback)
978-1-03-914799-7 (eBook)

1. *JUVENILE FICTION, VISIONARY & METAPHYSICAL*

Distributed to the trade by The Ingram Book Company

Printed in the USA
CPSIA information can be obtained
at www.ICGtesting.com
JSHW042302160624
64934JS00004B/105